Vasco, Our Little Panama Cousin

H. Lee M. Pike

Copyright © 2023 Culturea Editions
Text and cover : © public domain
Edition : Culturea (Hérault, 34)
Contact : infos@culturea.fr
Print in Germany by Books on Demand
Design and layout : Derek Murphy
Layout : Reedsy (https://reedsy.com/)
ISBN : 9791041829293
Légal deposit : July 2023

Vasco Our Little Panama Cousin

CHAPTER I.

HAPPY DAYS

IN young Vasco Barretas, who had both Spanish and Indian blood in his veins, there had been born a natural desire for excitement and adventure.

Just one thing equalled this desire. That was his dislike for work.

However, we must not blame him for that. His laziness was the result of training, or rather the lack of it. Necessities were few and easily obtained, and he had not learned to care for the luxuries of life.

On account of Vasco's fondness for bustle and excitement the time this story begins was most glorious for him. As his American cousin would say, "something was doing."

A successful revolution had just taken place in Panama.

A revolution was no new thing in the little strip of country that separates the Atlantic from the Pacific. Vasco's father had been through many such affairs. They had been nearly as regular as the rainy seasons.

Vasco did not understand all about it, yet even the boys in the streets knew that this revolution was different from any other.

There had been no bloodshed, but the results seemed likely to be very important to the country.

Do you want to know why?

Then listen to a little bit of history.

The State or Province of Panama, on the narrow bit of land connecting North and South America, had been a part of the country called the United States of Colombia.

The great republic to the north, the United States of America, wanted to dig a canal across Panama, but had been unable to get permission from Colombia. And so it looked as if there might be no canal—at least not in Panama.

The citizens of Panama were disappointed, for the digging of a canal through their country would bring to them many people and much wealth.

For this reason the leading men concluded that it was best to separate from Colombia, organize a government of their own, and come to an agreement with the United States. At the time this story opens the new government had just been set up, and its authority proclaimed.

But, it may be asked, what has all this to do with Vasco?

To begin with, Vasco's father, in private life a very ordinary citizen, who sometimes had been a waiter in a hotel and at other times the servant of an American engineer, was deeply interested in this latest revolution; for was he not an officer in the new National Guard,—Lieutenant Amadeo Barretas?

His position did not require much work, either of mind or body, but little Lieutenant Barretas could assume as much dignity as a seven-foot member of Napoleon's "Old Guard"—and more pomposity. When on parade he would strut about in his gaudy uniform with all the airs possible, and appear very serious—though to you he would have looked more silly than serious.

There was to be a grand review of the Panama "army." The soldiers were to parade through the streets of the city and be inspected by the commander-in-chief. Several officers of the United States army were to be guests of the Panama officials, and occupy a place on the reviewing stand.

Young Vasco meant to have a good sight of the parade. Surely he, the son of a lieutenant in the army, ought to have a place where he might see his father march by, and be able to add his voice to the thousands who would shout huzzas! But, for some reason, the officers in charge had neglected to invite him.

Vasco's home was on a side street in the poorer section of the city, so the soldiers would not pass by that place. How, then, could he get a good view of the parade?

Of course he could stand at the side of the street; but what chance would a small boy have in such a place as that?

Now Vasco was a boy of many resources, and it seemed to him that he might make use of the good nature of a young American friend.

Harlan Webster was the son of an American engineer who was in charge of work on the canal.

Mr. Webster had been for some time upon the Isthmus, and, unlike most of the Americans at work on the canal, he had brought his family, consisting of wife and son, to the city of Panama. They had now lived here over a year. During that time Harlan had learned a good deal about the country. He had also acquired some knowledge of Spanish, the language of the natives. In fact, it was said of him by his Panama friends that he could talk with the people more freely than many older foreigners who had been longer in the country.

The American boy knew many Panama lads, among them Vasco. "Lieutenant" Barretas, as he insisted on being called, had been in Mr. Webster's service at various times, and the two boys had thus become quite intimate and had taken many pleasure trips together.

Harlan was able to tell Vasco a good deal about Panama history. The stories about the buccaneers of old times, about the raid on the city of Panama, about Balboa and his adventures and discoveries, were more familiar to the American lad than they were to the Panama boy.

On the other hand, Vasco could give his friend much information about the every-day habits and customs of the people, and was able to take him to many points of interest. When it came to excursions by water or by land, Vasco was in his element. He could handle a boat with skill, he could swim like a fish, and he knew the windings and curvings of all the highways and byways of the city.

Straight to the hotel where the Webster family lived went Vasco this morning. This hotel was in the better part of the city, not far from the plaza, or great square.

"Hello, Harlan," said Vasco, after he had found his friend.

"Hello, Vasco."

"How would you like to see the great army parade this morning?"

"Fine," was the reply. "Where can we go to get a good view?"

"That's what I'd like to know. I don't want to stand in the crowd on the street, for I could never see anything that way."

"Let's see what my father can do to help us," said Harlan.

Mr. Webster, who was in an adjoining room, greeted his son's friend with a pleasant "Good morning" when the boys appeared before him. Seeing the eager, inquiring look on their faces, he asked what he could do for them.

"The Panama soldiers are going to parade to-day," said Harlan, "and Vasco is anxious to find a place where he can see them."

Mr. Webster smiled. He had an idea that Harlan was as anxious to get a view of the parade as was Vasco.

"Why don't you go into the cathedral and watch from the tower or from one of the upper windows?" asked Mr. Webster.

"None but officials and their families or others holding tickets can enter the cathedral till after the parade," replied Vasco, "and all entrances are guarded."

"If I tell you of a way to get into the cathedral, do you think you can remain within till the soldiers go by?" asked Mr. Webster.

"I'm sure we can," replied Vasco.

Mr. Webster, during his stay in Panama, had been able to pick up information about the place that even Vasco did not know, and he said to the boys, "You know where the old sea-battery is, on the other side of the plaza from the cathedral?"

"Yes," said the two boys together.

"Well, from that battery to the cathedral is an underground passage, built centuries ago to afford escape from the building. In times of revolution there was often danger even within its sacred walls."

Mr. Webster told the boys how they might find the entrance to the tunnel, and at once they were off to see for themselves. It took only a few moments to make their way from the hotel, down the street, across the plaza, and through a narrow alley to the old battery. Quickly they passed inside. Here Vasco was entirely at home, for many times he had wandered about the place, and with his friends had played hide-and-seek and other boyish games.

Notwithstanding this, it was hard for Vasco and Harlan to find the entrance to the underground passage. They opened many doors and wandered into several blind corridors. Vasco was almost ready to give up the search, but his American friend insisted on continuing. At last, behind a heap of old rubbish, they found the entrance they had so eagerly sought.

With a brave front the boys went into the dark passage. After going a few yards, they found themselves in complete darkness.

"I hope we shall not have to go far in this dark place," said Vasco.

Harlan pretended to give a careless reply, but, after he had stubbed his toes and scraped his shins on various obstacles in the path, he agreed that the adventure had its drawbacks.

Just then it occurred to Vasco that he had a supply of matches in his pocket. He scratched them one by one, thus faintly lighting the path. Then the boys were able to move forward more rapidly, and soon they came to what was evidently the foundation wall of the cathedral.

Through this wall was a low archway, which was blocked by what seemed to be a wooden barricade. There was no sign of a door.

"Well, we are really in trouble now," said Harlan.

"There's no doubt about that," replied Vasco as he put his shoulder to the partition. It did not budge, and the Panama lad was again inclined to give up the attempt to get into the cathedral.

"We may as well give up trying to get in this way," he said.

"Not yet," was Harlan's reply as they stood in the dark. "Strike another match, and let's see what this looks like, anyway."

Vasco scratched another match, and the two boys hastily looked over the stout planking. Not a crack nor a loose joint was to be seen.

Just before the match went out, Harlan glanced backward and spied upon the ground a stick of timber eight or ten feet long.

"Light another match," he shouted, darting toward the stick.

Lifting one end of it, he directed Vasco to take up the other end. It was not very easy for Vasco to do this and keep his match burning at the same time, but he managed to do so, though the light went out just as they reached the archway again.

"Let's batter down these old planks," said Harlan.

Together the boys began to pound at the barricade. Though Vasco was a small lad, compared with Harlan, his well-trained muscles, hardened and toughened by out-door life, came well into play.

Under such hammering as the boys were able to give, the planks began to loosen, and soon they made a hole large enough to crawl through.

Fortunately, this was in a remote part of the basement, and none heard the noise the boys had made. No one dreamed of putting a guard at this point. The entrance had been so long closed that nearly everybody had forgotten it.

Passing through, the boys found themselves in a small room which had been used as a storeroom.

"See the relics here," said Harlan.

"Mostly old rubbish, I guess," was Vasco's reply.

Whether relics or rubbish, the lads had no time to stop and examine the stuff. They made their way to a steep stairway, down which a ray of light came from a crack in the trap-door overhead.

Without a moment's delay Vasco and his friend mounted the stairs. With a strong push they put their shoulders to the heavy timbers of which the door was made. But the door had been too long settled in its place to yield at once to their pushing. By persistent effort, however, the door was moved. Slowly the boys raised it, looking carefully about as their eyes became accustomed to the light which flooded the room into which it opened.

It proved to be an anteroom on the main floor of the cathedral into which the boys had come. Vasco immediately recognized their surroundings. No one else was about, and the boys were able to make their way without challenge to the portico facing the plaza. Once mingled with the throng, there was no danger of any one interfering with their movements. It was taken for granted by the soldiers that Vasco and his friend had a right to be in the cathedral.

In truth, several of the guards were members of Lieutenant Barretas's company, and they knew Vasco, who had often visited their camp. They supposed, however, that the son of one of their officers had a right within the space reserved for guests. Vasco, in turn, knew who these particular soldiers were, and was not long making friends with them.

While waiting for the marching soldiers, Vasco told Harlan something of the history of the cathedral, which is built of yellow stone, with high Moorish towers.

As the boys looked up to the great dome, Harlan asked:

"What makes the dome sparkle so in the sunshine?"

"That's because of the hundreds of pearl shells that are stuck into the cement covering," replied Vasco.

"Do you know," continued Vasco, "that this great building was put up nearly one hundred and fifty years ago?"

"Yes," replied Harlan, "and I have heard that its builder was the first coloured bishop of this city."

"That is true," said Vasco, "and he was the son of a poor man who burned charcoal and then sold it from his back through the streets of Panama. The son was very kind to the poor people, and was noted for his charity."

"Yes," added one of Vasco's soldier acquaintances who stood near and overheard the talk, "and this cathedral is really a monument to the useful life of the bishop."

Further conversation was interrupted by the music of a brass band in the distance. The boys looked down the street by which the soldiers were to come to the plaza. In the distance they soon saw the uniforms of the officers followed by the long white lines of the soldiers.

Vasco's enthusiasm knew no bounds as the battalion wheeled into the plaza and passed by the cathedral with salutes for the onlookers. When he finally spied his father, Lieutenant Barretas, marching at the head of his company, Vasco was delirious with joy. To his mind, not even the general in command looked finer than did the little lieutenant—his father!

What cared Vasco if the lines of soldiers were not precisely straight? Even less did he mind Harlan's criticism and lack of admiration for the parade. Were not these soldiers enlisted in the service of his country, and were they not ready to lay down their lives in its defence?

Vasco's only wish was that he were old enough to join them and wear the uniform which to him seemed so glorious.

But, like all spectacles, grand as it seemed to Vasco, this one at last came to an end. The last flag had dipped before the reviewing stand, the last soldier had disappeared from the plaza, the last beat of drum was lost in the distance.

Meantime, the sun had risen high, and with its hot rays was driving to cover all the people of Panama. As was their usual custom, shopkeepers and market-men closed their doors at eleven o'clock and betook themselves to their homes to enjoy their noonday siesta.

Even the throngs of boys forsook their sports and disappeared from the streets, and Vasco and Harlan took their departure from the cathedral,— the latter to his cool room in the hotel, the former to his more humble home.

CHAPTER II.

ABOUT THE CITY

PERHAPS you would like to know more about Vasco Barretas—who he is, his home, his surroundings, his occupations, his ambitions. Of the two latter there is little to be said. Like many of the boys of Panama, he had no occupation—not even going to school—and no particular ambition. If any thought of the future ever did come into his mind, it was quickly forgotten for some pleasure of the moment.

It is fair to Vasco to say that it was not his fault that he did not attend school. Under the Colombian government there had been no public schools. There had been a few private schools under the care of the priests, but their equipment was very poor, and accommodations were limited.

Under the new government there was destined to be an improvement in this respect, and the year after the Panama Republic declared its independence, there were more than three thousand children in the schools, though previous to that there had been less than five hundred.

Vasco's home was a humble one, though it does not follow that it was unhappy. The contrary was the fact.

There were two children younger than Vasco,—Inez, his eight-year-old sister, and the little baby brother Carlos. The parents loved their children as fathers and mothers do everywhere, and were willing to sacrifice much for their welfare.

Both Lieutenant Barretas and his wife boasted of their Spanish ancestry, though they were of mixed descent, and there was evidenceof Jamaica negro blood in their features. Perhaps this accounted for Vasco's aversion to hard labour, though the strict truth of history does not reveal that the early Spanish discoverers were specially fond of manual toil.

Though Vasco's home could boast no luxuries, he had never seen the time when there was lack of food, and for clothing all he required was a pair of trousers and a shirt, both made of cheap linen cloth. Boy readers will realize the glorious possibilities in such a scanty attire.

Much of his time Vasco spent about the streets of the city, indulging in sports and games with boys of his own age. Often he went to the water-front and watched the loading and unloading of vessels. He specially liked to watch the fishermen as they came in with their little vessels, and brought their finny harvest ashore.

Fish are very abundant in Panama waters. The name of the city means "abounding in fish." Years ago many whales were caught off the coast, and whaling vessels were a common sight in the harbour.

At present, in addition to the edible fish, sharks are numerous in the Pacific near Panama. On one occasion Vasco had gone on a short fishing trip in one of the larger boats with the father of a boy friend. A shark was seen following the boat, and in consequence other fish were scared away.

To rid themselves of the unwelcome intruder the fishermen attached a piece of pork to a large fish-hook held by a small chain. To this was fastened a stout rope. No sooner was the baited hook cast overboard than the shark made a rush for it and swallowed it whole. When he found he was caught, there was a terrible lashing of the water, the shark leaping bodily into the air and vainly snapping his teeth again and again upon the chain.

After the fish had become pretty well exhausted, the men drew him on board the boat, but not without a fierce struggle. Soon he was killed, though not without much unnecessary torture.

Often Vasco wandered into the market district of the city. Many of the vendors of vegetables, fruits, and provisions occupied the narrow sidewalks, displaying their wares in full view of the passers-by.

At other times Vasco would spend hours under the shady palms in the great plaza watching the passing to and fro of all classes of people,—some on foot, some in carriages, some mounted on donkeys, and occasionally a military officer on horseback. When one of the latter came in sight, Vasco, with scores of other boys, would run a long distance to keep watch of the fine figure in such an abundance of gold braid.

The water-sellers, with their little carts drawn by wobegone-looking donkeys, were always an object of interest to Vasco. He felt that it would be almost as much fun to ride about on a water-cart all day as to be a soldier.

Among the buildings within Vasco's vision as he sat in the plaza was the Cabildo, or town hall, which is the Independence Hall of Panama, for here was signed the Declaration of Independence from Spain. Naturally the place is an object of much reverence to the natives. Near by is the Bishop's Palace, an imposing structure where much important Panama history has been made. At the present time the street floor is occupied by the great Panama Lottery Company. Let us hope that some day the people of that country will be delivered from this national shame, and the lottery banished.

Sunday evenings there was always a band concert in the plaza, and Vasco never failed to be present. Generally he took with him hissister Inez, and sometimes his mother, with little Carlos, would accompany them. This was always a joyful occasion, for Vasco liked nothing better than to hear the music and to watch the continual passing of the people.

CHAPTER III.

A TRIP TO OLD PANAMA

THOUGH Vasco had explored nearly every nook and corner of the city in which he had lived, he had never visited what was called Old Panama.

You must understand that the Panama of to-day is not on the site of the original city. The present city was built after the former one had been destroyed by the buccaneers. Of them you may learn something further on.

The so-called "modern" Panama was founded in 1673. As protection from pirates and buccaneers a high stone wall was built around the city, which cost over eleven million dollars. That seems to us an enormous sum, and to the people of those days it was fabulous. It gives some idea of the vast wealth that must have been stored in the city to admit of such an outlay for its protection. Few traces of this wall now remain. As civilization has advanced, and life and property have become safer, it has gradually been torn down.

One day, not long after the great military review, Vasco was down at the water-front watching the fishermen unloading their boats. As it happened, he fell in with Enrique Mendoza, in whose father's boat he had witnessed the capture of the shark.

Enrique, as well as Vasco, was always looking for some new adventure. At this time he hailed his friend with a glad shout, and asked:

"What do you say, Vasco, to a trip over to Old Panama to-morrow? Father will let us take a small boat he is not using, and we can go part of the way in that."

Vasco was much pleased at the invitation, but was in doubt as to whether it were perfectly safe for them to go without some one for protector and guide, as he had heard many disquieting stories about the old city.

"Have you ever been over there?" he asked Enrique.

"Many times."

"Do you know the way about?"

"Of course I do. I have often been there with father. Besides, there's an old friend of his who lives in a hut near the ruins, and he will be glad to show us about."

When Vasco heard the last statement, he hesitated no longer. "I'll go, then," he said. "I have never been there, and I should like to see what the place looks like. What do you say to asking my American friend Harlan to go with us?"

"That will be fine. The boat will carry three all right, and we will have all the jollier time."

Enrique had never seen Harlan Webster, but he had heard Vasco talk about him, and was greatly pleased at the thought of having him along on this trip. He had seen and heard enough of the Americans about the city to know that they were very active and enthusiastic. So he felt certain that this American boy would add to the fun of the excursion.

"All right, then," said Vasco. "We'll start early to-morrow morning. What time do you say?"

"Six o'clock won't be too early. It will take at least three hours to get over there. That will give us a little time to look around before the middle of the day, when it will be too hot to move about. Then in the afternoon we can search among the old ruins awhile, starting for home in season to get here before dark."

This plan suited Vasco, and he took leave of Enrique, saying that he would see Harlan sometime during the day. He had little doubt that the young American would go with them.

As the day was now well advanced, though, Vasco first made his way home, when for several hours he remained within doors. He told his mother of his plans for the next day, to which she made no objection. She rarely interfered with his movements, except that sometimes she asked him to do some chores about the house, and occasionally required him to look after Inez and his baby brother while she was away on an errand.

In the latter part of the afternoon Vasco went to see if Harlan could go with him the next day. It didn't take long to give the invitation, and it took Harlan even less time to accept it, so far as he was concerned.

"Wait a moment, though," he said to Vasco. "I must ask my mother if she is willing for me to go with you."

To Vasco this seemed unnecessary. He never thought of having to ask his mother about such things. But he had known Harlan long enough to learn that American ways, especially so far as boys were concerned, were different from Panama customs.

The American boy immediately went to his mother and told her what he wanted. At first she was inclined to object to his making this trip with only two other boys for companions, but his arguments and persuasions finally overcame her scruples, if not her fears, and he secured her consent.

Back to Vasco he hurried and told him the welcome news.

"Remember, now," said Vasco as he took his leave, "and be at the beach near the Panama Railroad pier at six o'clock sharp."

"I surely will. Good night," was Harlan's reply.

Both boys retired in good season that evening, to get well rested for their early start.

At dawn next day Vasco sprang out of bed. He was not concerned about the weather, for this was the dry season of the year, when for months no water falls, and there was no danger of rain preventing the day's outing.

Quickly he ate the breakfast his mother provided, and many minutes before the appointed time was on his way to the meeting-place. Though the first on the scene, he did not have to wait long for the other two boys. Enrique was the second to arrive, and shortly afterward Harlan made his appearance.

Harlan was glad to meet Enrique, and felt sure that if his mother could have seen the sturdy brown fisher-lad getting the boat ready she would have had no concern for their safety. All three boys were familiar with boats, though of course Harlan's acquaintance was with less rudely built craft than the one in which they were to cross the bay.

Each boy had brought along fruit for lunch. In addition, Vasco had some hard-boiled eggs, wrapped in corn-husks, as sold in the market. Eggs are not bought by the dozen in Panama, but by the pair. The boys expected either to catch fish or to get some from Juan, Enrique's friend who lived in the hut near the old city.

Soon they got under way in the little boat, with its sail spread wide to catch the light morning breeze. Enrique was at the rudder and Vasco acted as lookout at the bow, while Harlan made himself as comfortable as possible midway. All of them hugely enjoyed the sail across the bay.

Old Panama is only about four miles northeast of the present city in a straight line, but as the boys went, partly by water and partly on foot, they had to cover a much longer distance. That did not trouble them, however, especially while in the boat.

After sailing about an hour, a landing was made at Point Paitillo, which forms the protection for the upper side of the Bay of Panama. The boat was safely drawn up to shore and made fast to a huge boulder by a long line.

As the tide was high when they landed, they knew there was no danger of the boat's going adrift later in the day. In fact, as the tide receded it left the craft high and dry upon the shore. At Panama the tide has a rise and fall of about twenty feet.

The boat secured in its position, the boys took up their way afoot. They passed along the rocky shore, through some swampy lowland and over broad green fields, crossing many little brooks and rivulets.

To Harlan especially this walk was delightful. He greatly admired the park-like trees and shrubs, the luxuriant tropical vegetation, the beautiful scenery, fleeting glimpses of city and sea, and over all the clear blue southern sky.

After awhile the boys came to Algarrobo River, which empties into the sea close beside the ruins. The stream was spanned by an old stone bridge, built over 350 years ago. Across this they made their way and came in sight of the old city—or what was visible in the bewildering mass of tropical vegetation.

They did not immediately go into its depths, however, but, led by Enrique, sought out the hut of Juan, who lived a hermit life on the border of this city, where years ago there had been a great tide of humanity, and where ambition, avarice, gaiety, luxury, once had full sway, but now was only a memory. Where once thousands of people had thronged, now the only living things were serpents, alligators, iguanas, pumas, and such.

The boys were fortunate in finding Juan at home, and as it was now well toward the middle of the day, they were glad to get into the shelter of his little thatch-roofed hut, and rest their weary limbs after the long walk.

CHAPTER IV.

STORY OF THE BUCCANEERS

ENRIQUE'S friend Juan was a fine specimen of the Panama Indian. He was straight, clean-limbed, big-boned, well-shaped. His long, coarse, straight black hair hung loosely upon his shoulders. He was not very tall, but outdoor life had made him nimble and active and strong, and Harlan especially admired his athletic appearance.

Indians of unmixed blood are a rarity in Panama now, and Juan was exceedingly proud of the fact that no Spanish or negro blood flowed in his veins. This, too, probably accounted for his living alone. He was a member of the Tule or San Blas tribe of Indians, which not many years ago lived on the Atlantic coast of Panama, peaceably pursuing an honest, industrious life, occupied in fishing, hunting, farming, and sometimes trading.

Juan knew well what his ancestors had suffered from the Spaniards centuries ago, and how much it had cost to resist successfully their attacks. In consequence, he had no love for the white man. His hatred, however, did not include everybody, and he was on terms of close friendship with Enrique's father, who often marketed the fish Juan caught.

The Indian met Enrique and his companions with a smile, his even white teeth gleaming between his thin lips. He gave them a warm welcome, and invited them into the shelter of his hut, and the boys were very glad to accept his hearty hospitality.

"We have come to visit the old city," said Vasco, "and Enrique said you would be glad to show us about and tell something of its history."

"Yes, yes, but not now. Sun too hot. Go in and lie down. By and by we go to see the ruins."

Within the hut swung a hammock, which was generously given up to Harlan, while Vasco and Enrique made themselves comfortable on a rude grass couch covered with skins.

Meanwhile Juan set about, in his deliberate way, to prepare a meal for his visitors.

"Doesn't it seem strange," said Harlan to his companions, "that this place where there were once so many people should now be deserted?"

The American boy, though as full of fun as any lad, had a poetic nature, and in quiet moments was either building air-castles or dreaming over past events. The historic associations of this place brought to his mind much that he had read of the early visits of the Spaniards and of the bold buccaneers who followed in their trail.

Harlan's question had not much meaning either to Enrique or to Vasco, for in fact they knew much less about the history of the country and of their ancestors than did their American friend. But Vasco had enough curiosity to be interested in Harlan's question and the thought that might be behind it.

"Were there, then, very many people living here?" he asked.

"Yes, indeed, thousands and thousands. After his discovery of the Pacific Ocean Balboa founded the city, and thousands of Spanish countrymen flocked to the place in search of gold."

Harlan came very near saying something about their treatment of the native Indians, but he happened to think that Vasco and Enrique were both descendants of these same conquerors, and he was wise enough to hold his tongue.

"Many of the Spaniards," he continued, "succeeded way beyond their wildest dreams, and right here where you see these old ruins they were able to pile up a big lot of gold."

"If they became so rich," asked Vasco, "how did it happen that the city was deserted and fell to ruin?"

"Oh, that is a long story, and I am not sure that I could tell it very well, either," replied Harlan.

"There's plenty of time before Juan will have dinner ready," broke in Enrique, "and I am sure we would both like to hear how Old Panama was destroyed. You may be certain that not many boys in this country know the story, and it will give us something to brag about."

"Well, then," began Harlan, "you must know that for many years your ancestors and mine quarrelled, particularly over the control of the sea and its commerce. It was a long fight between the English and the Spanish, and it was a bitter one, too. Millions of dollars were spent, and blood — well, that flowed in rivers.

"In the search after wealth in the new world, the old rivalry between Spanish and English continued, and I guess that when it came to a fight neither side stopped to ask which was right or wrong. The men who sailed the ships on both sides were nothing but a set of pirates, and the governments at home didn't much care what the sailors did to their enemies.

"Thus it came about that a fierce and strong band of buccaneers, under Henry Morgan, was allowed to attack the Spanish vessels even at times when the nations were supposed to be at peace, though of course with no direct authority. It was this Morgan and his blood-thirsty cutthroats who destroyed the old city of Panama."

"How did you learn all this?" interrupted Vasco. "I have lived here all my life and never heard about this Morgan, though I have heard my father say that some of his ancestors were among those who lost life and property when the city was destroyed."

"Oh," said Harlan, "some things I learned in history at school, but a great deal I got from books of adventure that father has given me. If you only could read English I would lend you some of them, and you would find out much more than I can possibly tell you.

"But let me tell you about Morgan and his men. The old pirate chief himself was a Welshman, and if I remember correctly his father was a respectable farmer.

"The son didn't love the quiet life of a Welsh farmer, and so he left home when quite young. He joined the crew of a merchant vessel, and sailed for Barbados.

"Here he had very bad luck, which no doubt was partly the cause of his awful cruelty to his enemies in later years. He fell into the hands of the Spaniards and was sold into slavery."

"I'm mighty glad there are no slaves now," broke in Enrique. "I've heard my father tell some things about the way they lived, and it must have been terrible."

"It surely was," replied Harlan, "and yet the conditions of slavery with which your father is familiar were as nothing compared with the sufferings of slaves in Morgan's time. Probably his case was no better than others, but, as matters turned out, he succeeded after a time in getting his freedom. I can't tell you just how this was brought about, though I am sure his great strength and daring must have had much to do with it.

"Morgan next went to Jamaica, where he joined a band of pirates—mostly English and French—who attacked the Spanish treasure-ships in these waters. You can easily imagine that Morgan's part in this business wasn't small. He never thought of such a thing as mercy. The crews of captured ships who weren't killed in the battles had to walk the plank.

"Fortune favoured Morgan, and, unlike most of his companions, he saved his booty, and in a little while was able to buy a ship. In this vessel he had as villainous a body of men as ever walked the deck.

"With his ship he joined other pirate captains, and it was not long before he was in command of a fleet of fifteen vessels, with over five hundred men,—men who were not afraid of anything, and who did dreadful things wherever they went.

"With the constant additions to their force, the buccaneers began to spread out. They were not satisfied with capturing ships and killing their crews, but began to go upon the land, and a good many native and Spanish settlements in the West Indies and on the shore of South or Central America suffered. Wherever the pirates suspected Spanish treasure might be stored, they were sure to make their appearance, sooner or later. Town after town was captured and destroyed, and everything of value carried away."

"But what has all this to do with Panama?" asked Vasco, who, though interested in Morgan's history, was anxious to learn about the destruction of the city.

"I'm coming to that very soon," replied Harlan. "After a time Morgan and his men began to wonder if they could not capture Panama, which was then the chief city of all this region, and was famous everywhere for its vast wealth. And, as so often happens, the stories about its wonders far exceeded the reality.

"The inhabitants did not dream that the buccaneers would ever dare to attack Panama, fortified as it was, and defended by Spanish soldiers. But they didn't know much about the spirit which was in Morgan and his men, and they didn't realize to what the greed for gold would lead.

"To make a long story short, Morgan decided to attack Panama. By this time he had twelve hundred followers. Landing about forty miles from the city, with only a small supply of provisions, they took up their long march through forests and over the mountains and across the streams. They could not move very fast, and the men were nearly starved. I remember reading in some book, that at nightfall often the happiest man in the company was the one who had saved from his breakfast a small piece of rawhide on which to make his supper."

Vasco, who could make good use of anything eatable at any time, and who even now was wondering if Juan had dinner nearly ready, could not restrain an exclamation at this statement. "How could they live on that sort of stuff?" he asked.

"I don't know, myself," replied Harlan, "but we are told that the skins were first sliced, then dipped in water, and afterward beaten between stones. The morsel would then be broiled, cut into bits, and deliberately chewed, with plenty of cold water to wash it down.

"In addition to the danger of starvation, the pirates were in constant fear of ambuscades. The Spaniards, who knew of their approach, sent out parties of soldiers to meet them and hinder their march, though the defenders of Panama knew very well that they would lose a pitched battle.

Consequently they confined themselves to attacks from the cover of the dense forests, and in this way many a buccaneer was killed."

"Weren't the Englishmen able to find anything to eat while on the way?" asked Enrique.

"Very little indeed," replied Harlan, "until the ninth day, when they came to the outskirts of this city. What they saw there was very pleasing to these hungry men. On the broad, level land the other side of that bridge we just crossed were great herds of cattle."

"I'll wager they made a rush for them," said Vasco.

"They did, you may be sure," continued Harlan, "and so hungry were the men that they would hardly stop even to cook the meat.

"Their hunger satisfied, Morgan and his men moved on, and very soon caught a glimpse of the roofs and towers of the city. Then what a shout went up! The pirates, tired as they were, tossed their caps in the air and rushed forward with cheers. Drums were also beaten, and the invaders acted like crazy men at the thought of securing the rich treasure that lay in the city before them.

"Many of them wished to charge on the city and capture it at once, but their leader gave wiser counsel, and the pirates went into camp for the night, intending to move forward early in the morning."

"I should think the pirates would have been afraid to attack the city," said Vasco, "for there must have been many Spanish soldiers on guard there."

Probably Vasco had a higher opinion of Spanish bravery than did Harlan, but the young American gave no hint of his real thought. He simply said: "The pirates were the most desperate men on earth, and in their position it was win or die, for they could expect no quarter, and could not retreat over the path by which they had come.

"It is true," continued Harlan, "that the Spaniards greatly outnumbered the buccaneers, and they tried all sorts of schemes to defend the city. Among other things, they collected a great herd of bulls and drove them into the pirates' ranks with the hope that such disorder would be created as to make easy the enemy's destruction.

"But all that could be done in defence was useless against the villains who were greedy for gold. No mercy was shown, and death was the lot of all on either side who fell into the hands of their foes.

"After fierce fighting, which continued several days, Morgan and his men got into the city. Immediately the search for treasure was begun. Every house and building was ransacked, and if any inhabitant dared to resist, his life was immediately taken. Even helpless women and children were not spared."

"I don't see why they killed those who were unable to resist them," said Vasco.

"One reason why the pirates were so merciless was because of their disappointment. Though they did find vast stores of silver and gold, in many houses they were unable to find anything of value. This was because some of the people who lived in the city had hidden their treasure — in many cases burying it deep in the ground."

"That is so," interrupted Enrique, "and I have heard my father tell of seeing people come here to dig for buried gold. I never heard, though, that any one found much."

"Let Harlan go on with his story," said Vasco, sharply. "I want to hear how Morgan succeeded. Besides, I'm beginning to get hungry."

"There isn't much more to tell," said the young American. "When the pirates had finished their hunt they set fire to the city. At the same time they went on killing the people. Special vengeance was visited on the priests, for the robbers had been unable to find the great store of plate which the Church was supposed to possess.

"Morgan stayed here four weeks, taking everything of value, both on land and in the harbour. It is said that when he finally left the place it took one hundred and seventy-five mules to carry the plunder."

"What became of Morgan finally?" asked Vasco.

"Soon after his capture of Panama, I believe," replied Harlan, "he was appointed by King Charles the Second of England as deputy governor of Jamaica. Afterward King James the Second removed him and threw him into prison for his crimes."

"And good enough for him!" was Vasco's comment.

Just at this time Juan appeared in the doorway of the hut. "Come, boys, let's have something to eat," he said.

That was an invitation none of them cared to refuse, and they responded as only three hungry boys could.

Outside on a rude bench was spread the fresh fish that Juan knew so well how to cook over his camp-fire, together with Vasco's boiled eggs, potatoes, plaintains, and all sorts of vegetables and fruit. The sail and the long walk had added zest to appetites always splendid, and the good things on the bench disappeared as if by magic.

"I must say," said Harlan, "that that's about the best tasting fish I ever ate. And I have eaten a good many kinds, too."

Juan, silent like most of his race, said nothing in reply to the compliment, but a significant look and a grunt of satisfaction showed that he appreciated the American boy's remark.

The boys finished their meal with generous mugs of hot cocoa. Juan was an expert in its preparation, but to his own particular draught he added a seasoning of chili pepper. This he drank boiling hot,—a process which would have terribly scalded the mouths and throats of his visitors, but the Indian swallowed the hot mixture without any trouble and with much satisfaction.

Vasco and his friends looked on in amazement, and were all the more surprised when Juan told them that in years gone by it was the fashion of his forefathers to sit upon the ground with open mouths while their squaws poured the boiling mixture down their throats.

Their generous dinner disposed of, Vasco suggested that they immediately begin the exploration of the old city. This was agreed to by the others, and under Juan's guidance they at once made their way into the dense jungle which had grown up about the ruins.

Neither of the Panama boys was very romantic in disposition, but Vasco could not help thinking of the pirates of whom Harlan had told,—how they had trod this very ground, and how back and forth Spaniards and buccaneers had swept in bloody battle. All the military ardour which had been born in his breast was aroused, and he even caught himself wishing that he had been there to help defend the city. Little did he realize how much less enchanting was the experience than the story.

It is not possible to describe all that the boys saw. As they wandered back and forth they imagined that here was a market-place, and there was the residence of some rich old Spanish trader. Over yonder was all that remained of a bishop's palace, and near by may have been the governor's abode.

The old cathedral was easily identified by the tower which still stands. Within its walls the boys went and gazed with awe upon the ancient altar on which Pizarro, the adventurous explorer and conqueror, had left an offering to the Holy Virgin before starting on his voyage to Peru.

Time passed swiftly, however, and it was Enrique who discovered that the sun was fast setting.

"We must soon be starting," he said to Vasco, "if we are to get home before dark."

Harlan, who overheard what Enrique said, was anxious to start immediately, for he knew his mother would be worried if he were late.

So bidding Juan good-bye and thanking him profusely for his kindness to them, the boys took up their homeward march across the old bridge and along the coast. Not so much time was spent on the way as in the morning, for now they were intent only on getting home.

The boat was found safely fast where they had left it, and, quickly spreading the sail, they were soon speeding across the blue waters of the bay. The sail was a delightful one, the cool breeze fanning their cheeks while the slanting rays of the sun cast a glory over the scene which subdued their boyish spirits and filled them with awe as they gazed about them.

Before long, however, they arrived at the water-front of the city. Here was a busy, bustling scene. A great steamer from San Francisco had arrived during the day, and a gang of negro labourers was busily transferring the freight from its capacious hold to the cars which stood alongside on the dock. On the other side of the Isthmus the process would have to be repeated in a reverse manner. The freight would be unloaded from the cars and shipped to New York, New Orleans, Liverpool, and other ports of the United States and Europe.

At the same time numerous small boats were drawn up near the beach, discharging fish, poultry, fruit, and various cargoes. Here the boys saw a sight which was new even to Vasco, though he had seen about everything that went on in Panama. A small schooner from up the coast had brought in a cargo of live pigs for the Panama market. The vessel was not made fast to a wharf and the pigs taken out over a gangplank, but it was moored as near the beach as safety would allow. Then the pigs were dumped overboard and compelled to swim for land, where they were caught. Later they would be slaughtered and their carcasses exposed for sale in the market-place.

The sight of the squealing, swimming pigs was very amusing to Vasco and Harlan, and they watched with glee the unloading of the whole boat-load before they went ashore.

"What queer-looking pigs those are!" said Harlan.

"Why?" Vasco asked.

"See how lean they are, and what long snouts they have!"

"Well, isn't that the way all pigs look?"

"Not up in my country," replied Harlan. "Those that I have seen were so fat that they could hardly move. These pigs are not at all like them; though I have heard that in the Southern States many of the wild hogs are thin and long-legged."

Soon the boys bade each other good night, and Vasco went to his home ready for the supper his mother had prepared for him. Not long afterward he went to bed, thoroughly tired, but very much pleased with his day's outing. If he dreamed at all that night there must have appeared a strange mixture of Spaniards and pirates and Indians and ruins and—pigs!

CHAPTER V.

AN EARTHQUAKE

"VASCO," called his mother to him early one morning a few days later, "I want you to get up and go to market for me."

"Oh, dear, I don't want to get up now," said Vasco.

"No matter," replied his mother, "you'll want something to eat by and by, so hurry up."

Vasco knew it was no use to protest further, and, as the process of dressing was a very short one with him, he soon was ready to do his mother's errand.

"What do you want me to get this morning?" he asked.

"I want you to get some potatoes and peas and rice and half a yard of beef," his mother replied, as she handed him a basket.

It sounds strange to hear about a yard of beef, doesn't it? Vasco did not think so, though, for in Panama beef, instead of being sold by the pound, is often cut into long strips and sold by the yard.

By the time Vasco was all ready to start his sister Inez was up.

"May I go with you?" she asked.

"Of course, if you want to. Come on."

So together they trotted out of the house and off to market.

Inez looked about her with wide-open eyes, for her visits to the market, especially in the early morning, had been very rare.

"See what a lot of donkeys standing over there," said the little girl, pointing across the street.

"Yes; they belong to the fruit-sellers you see here. The animals stand there all day long, and at night, when their masters and mistresses have sold all their stock, they ride home on the backs of the donkeys. Some of them go many miles into the country, too."

But other sights soon attracted Inez's attention, and the donkeys were forgotten.

Many of the buyers were women cooks dressed in red and yellow and green and bright colours of all sorts. They made the place look very brilliant.

Soon, however, Vasco had done his errands and with Inez hurried home for breakfast.

Sometimes, in the evening, Vasco would go out with his mother and Inez and little Carlos.

On Sunday evenings, as you have already learned, they went to the plaza and listened with rapt attention to the band concert.

Quite often, on these occasions, Vasco's father, the lieutenant, would have a leave of absence from his military duties, and would go with his family. Then Vasco was supremely happy, for he was extremely proud of the gorgeous uniform which his father wore, and felt as if some of the military glory were reflected upon him.

Since Panama had become an independent nation, much patriotic music had been played at these concerts, and the large crowds were always enthusiastic.

On one Sunday evening, soon after the boy's visit to Old Panama, all the members of the family except little Carlos were listening to Vasco's tales of the sights he had seen in the old city. He also was repeating the story of the buccaneers that Harlan had told him.

Lieutenant Barretas was especially interested in what Vasco said about the treasure buried amid the ancient ruins.

"Our ancestors," he said to his son, "were not the only ones who left their wealth buried in the ground about here. The pirates who so cruelly robbed the early settlers of the country often hid their ill-gotten gains in caves in the sand on the shore or upon some barren island. Then they sailed away, and sometimes never returned to secure their treasure. If the stories were to be believed, all we need to do to obtain untold wealth is to take picks and spades and turn up the earth along the coast of our country or on the islands near its shores.

"Years ago a good many people actually spent much time searching for hidden gold. I remember hearing my grandfather tell of a neighbour who formed one of a party that went to Cocos Island for such a purpose.

"It seems that many years before a dying pirate had confided to an old countryman, a carpenter by trade, that a vast store of gold was buried on Cocos Island."

"I have heard of that place," interrupted Vasco. "Some of the sailors whom Enrique and I know have mentioned it. The island isseveral hundred miles from Panama, and there are no people living on it."

"That is true," said the lieutenant. "Well, this carpenter was nearly mad with joy at the information the dying pirate gave him. He thought surely that his fortune was made. No more hard work for him! All he needed to do was to dig up the treasure, and for the rest of his life enjoy ease and freedom from care."

"I don't much blame him, father, do you?" asked Vasco.

"I can't say that I do," was the reply. "I'll admit I wouldn't mind digging up a pot or two of gold myself, though I don't believe that we take so much stock in the stories of hidden wealth as our fathers and grandfathers did.

"With this carpenter, however, it was a pretty serious question how he was going to get to Cocos Island and secure the treasure. He knew the island was a desert place and far from shore. It would be necessary to have a ship, a good store of provisions, and tools with which to do the digging, to say nothing of a company of men to help him. All this required much money, and our poor carpenter had none. But he was possessed of a large amount of courage and perseverance, and he managed after a time to enlist the help of men of means, who furnished the capital for the expedition.

"Many hardships were endured by the little band of men who made up the carpenter's company, but they finally arrived at the island.

"The pirate had not made very clear the exact location of the hidden gold, and as the island was covered with a dense growth of trees and vines, the search was a heartless task from the beginning. The men, however, got to work, and with picks and spades and gunpowder managed to uncover a large part of the island."

"And did they find the gold?" asked Vasco, his face now aglow with excitement.

"Not any," replied his father. "Several months they dug and blasted, but all in vain. No sign of chest, box, silver, or gold was found. Day after day the search continued. Finally the provisions became exhausted, the men grew disheartened, and a weary, disappointed company of men returned to Panama."

Just as Vasco's father finished his story a strange rumbling noise was heard. You would have wondered what it was, and perhaps have been a little frightened. The Barretas family, however, knew in a moment what had happened.

"An earthquake!" cried Vasco.

Even as he spoke two or three tiles fell from the roof into the street. A startling clatter breaking the stillness of the evening proved that the tiles had been shaken loose from neighbouring houses, also.

"We'd better get out quick," cried the lieutenant, and he made a dash for the door.

Vasco and his mother were more thoughtful about the younger children, and, while the mother rushed into the bedroom after Carlos, Vasco took Inez by the arm and followed closely on his father's heels.

In a moment the whole family was in the street.

"Get away from the house!" shouted Vasco's father. "The tiles are likely to fall upon you if you don't."

To the middle of the street they all dashed, where they were quickly surrounded by a noisy, chattering mob of men, women, and children.

Again the earth seemed to shake and to shiver, and the shrieks and moans of frightened women and children were accompanied by the sound of more falling tiles and cracking timbers.

The experience was truly fearful, even to the older and wiser ones. The terror of the young children was something to excite pity in the most hardened breast. It was only by the utmost efforts and constant reassurance that no harm would come to her that Vasco was able to quiet his sister Inez. Even after her cries had become stilled she trembled like a leaf.

Fortunately the shock was a light one and the shaking and trembling of the earth were soon over. Lieutenant Barretas and his family returned within their house none the worse for the adventure, and went to bed, but many of their neighbours lingered in the street for hours—some even until daylight, when the terror of the night was dissipated by the cheerful rays of the rising sun.

The earthquake had been a mild one compared with some instances of previous years. In September, 1882, the city had been visited in the night by a terrible shock. The darkness always adds intensely to the terror of the people. On this occasion men and women of all classes—high and low— had rushed to the street. Great hotels were emptied in a few moments, many guests not stopping even to put on clothing.

The great plaza was one vast mass of shouting, crying people, while the earth heaved and the air quivered as it had never done in the memory of the inhabitants. Many houses were ruined, much property destroyed, and it is said that some even died from fright.

At daybreak new courage revived the hearts of the people, but for several nights the plaza was occupied by tents and all sorts of rude shelters for thousands who dared not sleep in their houses.

CHAPTER VI.

A JOURNEY

A FEW days after the earthquake, early in the forenoon, there came a rap at the door of Vasco's home. Inez, always alert, ran to the door, and, throwing it open, saw Harlan Andrews standing there.

"Good morning, Inez," said the young American.

Inez had become quite well acquainted with Harlan because of his many visits to Vasco, and was always glad to see him. So she gave a cheerful smile and hearty response to his greeting, and invited him to enter.

"Is Vasco at home?" asked Harlan, as he came into the living-room.

"Yes, he is out in the courtyard. If you will sit down I will call him."

Harlan thought he was quite fortunate to find Vasco. Generally at this time of day he was out upon the streets with other boys of his age.

In a moment Vasco came into the house, and, boylike, Harlan stated his errand without any preliminary conversation.

"Father is going to make a trip to Colon in connection with his canal work, and will spend some time on the way, particularly at the Culebra cut. Perhaps, too, he will go up the Chagres River to the place where it is proposed to build the big dam. He is going to take me with him, and says I may invite you to go along."

"Oh, that will be fine!" exclaimed Vasco, and he fairly jumped up and down with glee. In fact, he was so overwhelmed by the thought of the proposed journey that he nearly forgot to thank Harlan for the invitation. When he did come to his senses, his gratitude was profuse, and his tongue could not begin to express his thoughts.

Then again, after a few moments, he remembered that this trip was for more than a day, perhaps for more than a week, and it might be necessary to consult his parents before accepting the invitation. At once he turned to his mother, who had overheard all the conversation.

"Are you willing I should go with Harlan?" Vasco inquired.

For a moment his mother did not reply, and the boy was very anxious for fear that when she did give her answer it might not be favourable.

Finally the señora said, "If your father has no objection, I think I am willing to let you go."

"Then I'll go now to ask him. Come on, Harlan," said Vasco.

The lieutenant was stationed in the city at this time, so the boys had not far to go. Vasco did not anticipate any great difficulty in gaining his father's consent to the journey. As the result proved, his hopes were well founded, for Lieutenant Barretas was quite willing his son should go anywhere, provided he was in Mr. Andrews's care.

"It's all right, then," said Harlan when the matter was decided. "Meet me at the railway station next Monday morning at eight o'clock." This was Friday.

For Vasco, the two days between Friday and Monday passed—oh, so slowly! It seemed as if they would never go by!

Meanwhile, his mother gave him a bit of information which later turned out to be of value. "You say you may go up the Chagres River?" she asked her son.

"Yes, so Harlan told me," was Vasco's reply.

"I have never told you that I have a brother living in that part of the country—your Uncle Francisco Herreras. The last I knew of him he had a plantation not far from Palo Grande. I hope, if you go near there, you may be able to call upon him. I am sure he will be very hospitable to you all."

At last Monday morning came. Very early Vasco awoke, ate the breakfast his mother made ready for him, and long before the hour appointed was ready to start for the railway station. He was so impatient to be on his way that he left home a full hour earlier than was necessary. Consequently, he had to wait a long time at the depot.

But time flies, even for the most impatient lads, and in due time Harlan and his father made their appearance.

"What do you think, Vasco?" said Harlan. "We are going to have a special train!"

"Where is it?" asked Vasco, who saw no sign of anything of that sort in the depot.

"Oh, it's not in here. It's outside in the train-yard. We are going out there to get aboard."

Vasco thought this a little strange, but felt that he could ask no questions. In a moment Mr. Andrews called to the boys to follow him, and led the way outside the station.

Directly they came in sight of an engine, to which was attached a box car and a flat car such as are ordinarily used for freight. On the flat car were fixed several seats, and an awning had been erected as protection from the fierce rays of the sun. In the box car were well-equipped bunks, where the members of the party might sleep at night when better accommodations were wanting.

"This is our special private car," said Harlan. "What do you think of it?"

"I think it will suit me all right," said Vasco.

Mr. Andrews explained to the boys that he was on a tour of inspection in connection with the canal work, and this train had been placed at his disposal. He was glad, in connection with his work, to give a pleasure trip to the boys. He hoped it might also prove an instructive and beneficial one to them.

While Mr. Andrews had been talking to the boys they all had climbed upon the flat car and taken seats. Then, with a wave of the hand to the engineer, the signal was given, the throttle opened, and the train began its journey.

Slowly it moved until away from the city, but when it had passed out upon the beautiful broad savannahs, or grassy plains, which lie near Panama it moved with greater speed. To Vasco it seemed very fast indeed, though it was far otherwise to Harlan, who had ridden on the rapid express trains in his own country.

As the train drew farther from Panama they came to a more hilly region. In turn they passed through Corozal, Rio Grande, Miraflores, Pedro Miguel, and Paraiso. Most of these places were small settlements. Near the little railway stations would be seen a few wretched houses. What few inhabitants were in sight appeared to be of native Indian descent and wandered about in scanty clothing, with no apparent occupation.

At Paraiso the train was run on to a side-track.

"We shall have to wait here awhile for the regular passenger-train for Panama City to pass us," said Mr. Andrews.

"How long shall we have to wait?" asked Harlan.

"Oh, I'm sure I don't know. The trains on this road come when they please and go when they get ready. You may as well take it easy till we can go on again."

"How long does it take to run across the Isthmus?" asked Vasco.

"Generally about three hours for the forty-mile trip, but as I just told Harlan, you can't be sure of anything on this road. They ought to give better service, for they carry nearly one hundred thousand people a year."

Fortunately our friends did not have to wait very long, and when they again had a clear track they proceeded on their way.

"It must have been a big job to build this road," said Vasco, as they rode on.

"Yes," replied Mr. Andrews, "it was a great triumph of American genius. During its construction multitudes of men were killed by the deadly fever, but finally Chinese labourers were imported and successfully completed the work, though even many of these Oriental coolies died."

The train whirled on through rocky hills and valleys luxuriant with tropical foliage. As it approached Culebra Mountain Vasco's eyes opened wide at the sights he saw. From the main track various spurs were laid, on which stood giant steam-shovels.

Pointing to one of them, Mr. Andrews said: "That scoop will dig out of the mountain a ton of earth at a time. Then it is swung around and its load emptied into a gravel-car. In this manner train-load after train-load is taken from the sides of the mountain each day and hauled away and dumped either into a valley or into the sea at Colon."

Vasco also saw large gangs of men at work on the side of the mountain. Most of them were negroes from Jamaica. As the boys watched them at their labour Harlan said to his friend: "Well, those fellows can't be accused of trying to work themselves out of a job. I reckon they would move livelier than that if they were at work on some of our American railroads."

CHAPTER VII.

CULEBRA

AT the Culebra station Mr. Andrews's train stopped. "Now, boys," he said, "it is nearly noon. We will see what we can get for dinner, and then I shall have to leave you to yourselves for the rest of the day. I have considerable business to which I must attend. All I ask is that you keep out of danger and show up at supper-time. We shall sleep in the car to-night and to-morrow go on our way to Colon."

"That will give us the whole afternoon to look about this place, and I think we can manage to see a lot in that time," said Harlan.

"I'm glad we're going to have some dinner first," said Vasco, "for I'm hungry."

"Come on, then," said Mr. Andrews, and he led the way to a large wooden shanty a few rods from the station. The building was dignified with the title of a "hotel," and served as a boarding-place for the American overseers of the gangs of men at work in the Culebra cut. Here the three sat down to a generous meal. There was not much style about it, but Mr. Andrews cared little for that, and certainly the boys were not fussy.

Dinner over, the boys were left to their own devices.

"I tell you what let's do," said Vasco. "We'll climb to the top of Culebra Hill this afternoon. We can get a splendid view of the country, and we can certainly get back in time for supper."

"That suits me," said Harlan.

At once they started. From the level of the railway tracks, the climb at first was up the steep and slippery banks that had been made by the steam-shovels. Many times the boys lost their foothold and slid backward, only to renew the struggle and clamber upward once more.

As they got higher up their progress was hindered by the dense undergrowth of shrubs and vines, so that they were obliged to make many a turn and twist in their path. In some places they could not get through the bushes, and had to tramp a long way around to gain a few yards toward the summit.

Finally their perseverance was rewarded, and they stood upon the top of the great hill. Such a scene was spread before them as is seldom witnessed. In the immediate foreground far below them they could see the hundreds of men at work. They looked hardly larger than ants and not half so active. Here also they saw the labourers' camp,—a collection of rude shanties closely huddled together.

Looking farther out, the scene was more attractive. Down through the valleys the rich-looking tropical foliage made a picture no artist could reproduce, and even boyish spirits were subdued as Vasco and Harlan gazed about them. In the distance ridge upon ridge of hills arose, adding grandeur to the magnificent view.

Awe-inspiring as was the handiwork of nature spread before them, to these boys the great work which man was here undertaking seemed even more wonderful. The scores of steam-shovels in sight were scooping up tons upon tons of earth every hour. Vasco could hardly believe it when Harlan told him that it would take years to complete the work of cutting through the mountain. The great valleys in the locality would be entirely filled with the earth, and thousands of car-loads were to be hauled to Colon and dumped into the Atlantic.

Little did those early Spanish explorers and English buccaneers who travelled over this country imagine that great ships—many times larger than any they ever dreamed of—would be sailing through this mountain.

Vasco could hardly fancy such a thing now, but Harlan, with sublime confidence in American skill and force, had perfect faith in the early completion of the Panama canal. Certainly here before him was splendid evidence of American purpose.

When the boys had become thoroughly rested after their hard climb, and had concluded that there were no more worlds to conquer in this direction, they began to think of returning to the camp. The declining sun also reminded them that it was time to be on the move. Possibly, also, a vigorous appetite added to Vasco's zeal for the return journey. At any rate, he said to Harlan: "What do you say to a race to the railway station?"

This suggestion suited the American boy, and in a trice they were off,—running, jumping, sliding, tumbling, dodging, twisting, and turning in the race for the foot of the hill. There was just enough danger in it to add interest to the contest.

In the end Vasco won, though Harlan pressed him closely all the way. Several times, indeed, he seemed to gain the lead, his shrewdness and good judgment proving nearly a match for the sturdy limbs and deep breath of his opponent.

The race over, the boys wandered about watching the shifting gravel-trains, the giant steam-shovels in operation, the hundreds of men at work, and toward the close of the day returned to the car.

Here they found Mr. Andrews, and with him went to supper. At an early hour thereafter they turned into their bunks in the "sleeping-car," where, with nets protecting them from hungry mosquitos and other insects, they soundly slumbered through the night.

Early in the morning the three travellers were again on their way, for Mr. Andrews was anxious to get to Colon. They did not even go to the "hotel" for breakfast, but ate some canned food which had been brought along in the "sleeper." Taking his meals on a railway train was a novelty for Vasco,—more so than a dinner in the finest Pullman dining-car would have been to Harlan. None the less, Harlan enjoyed the novelty of the situation as much as his Panama friend.

Breakfast eaten, the boys devoted themselves to watching the scenery along the route. The forests through which they passed abounded in all sorts of bird and animal life.

As the train whirled along, the boys caught glimpses of wild turkeys, bright-coloured macaws and parrots, as well as of innumerablesmaller birds. Monkeys were seen darting about amidst the foliage. Once also a drove of peccaries was seen scuttling away through the undergrowth.

These little animals resemble the Virginia wild hog in shape, and are black in colour. The natives of Panama kill them for food.

The trees were innumerable in variety. Besides the ordinary oak, cedar, beech, and ash, were seen teak, rosewood, mahogany, and ebony in abundance. When they become more accessible, these will bring fortunes to their possessors.

Vasco called particular attention to the macaw-trees. He said they bore a very palatable fruit about the size of a pear, with a stringy covering and a stone in the centre. In old times the Indians were very fond of it, and recklessly cut down thousands of trees for the sake of the fruit alone. They used the black and very hard wood for arrow-heads.

As the train rolled into Obispo, the travellers got their first glimpse of the Chagres River, which forms such an important link in the construction of the canal.

CHAPTER VIII.

BALBOA

ALONG the river's bank the train sped. As it approached Matachin Mr. Andrews pointed to a high hill not far away.

"Do you know what hill that is?" he asked Vasco.

"No, sir."

"Well, you ought to, for it is the spot of greatest historic interest in your country. Cerro Gigante, or Big Hill, is its name, and from its summit was gained the first sight of the Pacific Ocean. Do you know who the discoverer of that ocean was?"

"Yes, sir, it was Balboa, who also helped to build the city of Panama. I have heard my father speak of him."

"Balboa's life was full of adventures," said Mr. Andrews, "and included many dramatic incidents, but none equalled in intensity the moment when he first sighted the broad blue Pacific, which he called the 'Sea of the South.' At the head of a little band of tired Spaniards he toiled up that hill. The vision that met his eyes amply repaid him for all the hardships and privations he had suffered—and they had not been few."

Vasco's interest was now thoroughly aroused, and he asked Mr. Andrews to tell him more about Balboa and his adventures.

"Perhaps I do not know very much about Balboa, but I am very glad to tell you what I can.

"If I remember correctly, he was born about 1475 in Spain. So you see he was just coming to young manhood when the wonderful discovery of a new world by Columbus thrilled every Spanish heart.

"Balboa was of noble parentage, though his family had become poor. A few years after the discovery of America he sailed with Bastides and coasted up and down this country.

"At first he was very successful in his ventures, but on account of the sinking of his ship he settled in Santo Domingo, and undertook to make his living by farming. In this he failed. Soon his savings were spent, and he found himself in debt. This was a serious matter for Balboa, as under Spanish law debtors were shown very slight consideration."

"Why didn't he run away?" asked Vasco.

"That is just what he wanted to do," replied Mr. Andrews, "but it was almost impossible to get away from the island unobserved. Finally, however, he made a desperate effort. He placed himself in a cask and caused it to be carried from his farm on board a ship that was ready to sail for South America.

"When well out to sea, he appeared to the captain, who at first was exceedingly angry. The captain relented, however, after he had heard Balboa's story, and allowed the fugitive to remain with him.

"Later, a wealthy friend supplied funds for an expedition of which Balboa was the head. At first he was unsuccessful and results were not promising, but on a visit to the Isthmus much wealth was secured, and Balboa's great success — the discovery of the Pacific — was attained.

"The building of the city of Panama soon followed. It was from that place that Pizarro, one of Balboa's companions, a few years later, sailed for Peru, whence such fabulous wealth was carried back to Spain. You saw in the ruins of the old cathedral the altar where Pizarro offered sacrifice to the Holy Virgin."

Here Mr. Andrews concluded his story, and Harlan added:

"You did not tell Vasco that Balboa made friends with an Indian chief on the Isthmus, and married his daughter. More than that, unlike a lot of Spanish explorers, he really loved his Indian wife and remained true to her — so true, in fact, that he afterward lost his life on her account."

"And was Balboa finally killed, then?" asked Vasco.

"Yes; he was executed by order of a jealous governor of the Isthmus," replied Mr. Andrews.

"That seems strange, after all he had done for his country," said Vasco.

"I know it does," was Mr. Andrews's answer; "but that was the way Spain often dealt with her adventurous explorers. Many of them deserved their fate much more than Balboa, though."

While Mr. Andrews had been telling the story of Balboa, the train continued to roll on. Gorgona, San Pablo, and Tavernilla were passed in succession. Bohio was a special point of interest, for here, as Mr. Andrews told the boys, the canal is to enter the artificial lake to be formed by a great dam. When complete, there will be a broad, deep body of water seven miles in length, affording room for anchorage as well as for navigation.

Gatun was the next place of importance, and not long after the train passed through Monkey Hill, a suburb of Colon, and finally into the city of Colon itself.

CHAPTER IX.

COLON

ARRIVING in Colon, as they did about midday, the boys had little desire to go sightseeing immediately. The weather was too hot and uncomfortable. They ate dinner at a hotel with Mr. Andrews, but it was decided to sleep on board their car every night. It was as comfortable as any place they were likely to find.

As the car was side-tracked upon the railway dock, they had the full benefit of the sea breezes, and during the remainder of that day Vasco stayed upon the car with Harlan, watching the waves roll in from the broad Atlantic.

Colon is situated on the extreme point of land between Limon and Manzanillo Bays. There is really little harbour, and in case of severe storm little protection for shipping.

"Sometimes there are terrible storms here," said Harlan, "when the waves come in with tremendous force."

"I can see along the shore," said Vasco, "where much damage has been done."

"That is not the worst, either," continued Harlan. "During these storms many lives have been lost. It was only a little while ago that one of the most severe of these 'northers' attacked this coast. Father was telling me about it, as he happened to be in Colon at the time.

"Three steamships put to sea for safety and remained away three days. The gunboat Dixie also ran out as quickly as it could to escape the danger. Not a vessel of any kind remained in the harbour except two schooners in the slips close by this station. They were tied by a number of cables at a sufficient distance from the piers to prevent damage from the pitching and rolling. They couldn't get away, and rode out the gale.

"Great waves rolled directly into the harbour, breaking over the water-front, and even the streets were filled with water. From a number of houses the people had to get out."

"It doesn't look now as if the sea ever could do such harm, does it?" said Vasco.

"Indeed it does not. It is very calm and gentle this afternoon. Father told me that one of the plans in connection with digging the canal is the building of a big breakwater here."

"If that is done the harbour will be much safer, won't it?" asked Vasco.

"Yes, and the entrance to the canal will be less likely to suffer damage in a storm," said Harlan.

"It looks as if a number of old wrecks were strewn along the shore now," said Vasco, indicating at the time numerous hulks thatappeared just above the surface of the water along the shore.

"Those are relics of the French effort to dig a canal here. Scores of scows were built by the De Lesseps company, and when work was given up they were left to decay and sink."

"Why didn't some one take care of them?" asked Vasco. "They must have cost a lot of money."

"That's one of the questions no one can answer, any more than one can tell why so many costly engines and steam-shovels and dredges were left to rust and grow useless by exposure."

"I remember we saw some of them near the railway. A good many were more than half-buried in the sand, too," said Vasco.

Thus the boys whiled away the afternoon, and at night, with Mr. Andrews, turned into their berths in the "sleeper."

In the morning, after an early breakfast, the boys started to explore the town. They found that most of the buildings were mere wooden shanties.

"This city makes me think of some of the beach resorts in my country," said Harlan. "The houses are just such flimsy affairs."

There were no cellars, and the houses were set up on stakes. The streets hardly deserved the name, and were littered with all kinds of dirt and filth.

Even Vasco, who could not be accused of being particular, said that he much preferred to live in his own city of Panama.

After dinner, during the hottest part of the day, the boys indulged in a siesta, and later took a walk to Coconut Point, where the French had built a number of fine houses, and cleared and drained the land to make healthful surroundings for the officers of the canal company.

One specially elegant house was built for the sole use of De Lesseps — and he occupied it less than one hour. The whole situation and surroundings were ideal and a splendid reminder of the extravagance of the French canal company.

At night, when the boys returned to their car, Mr. Andrews told them that he had completed his business in Colon, and that they would start on the return trip in the morning.

CHAPTER X.

UP THE CHAGRES RIVER

AFTER another night on the "sleeper" in Colon, Mr. Andrews and the boys started on their return journey. The trip was made as far as Obispo without special incident. Here a halt was made and the train shifted to a side-track. Mr. Andrews was obliged to inspect the site of a proposed dam near Alhajuela. This was about ten miles northwest of Obispo, and the journey would have to be made by a boat and on foot.

It was too far to go that day, so Vasco suggested that they go to Palo Grande and hunt up his uncle, Francisco Herreras. "I am sure," said the boy, "that he will give us all a hearty welcome and be glad to provide shelter and food for us."

"Let's go there," said Harlan to his father. "It will be lots more fun than staying here to-night. It will give us more chance to see the country, too."

Vasco's suggestion was favourably received by Mr. Andrews, who proceeded at once to carry the plan into effect.

On going to the nearest river landing-place to see if he could find a boat and men to row them up-stream, he met with unexpected good fortune. Two natives, who had come down to Obispo with a boat-load of bananas, were just ready to return, and were glad to earn an extra sum by taking along three passengers.

The boat in which passage was secured was a large flat-bottomed affair, suitable for navigation of the shallow stream. On the way up many similar boats were seen, also rude canoes propelled by single persons.

Vasco and Harlan, full of curiosity as boys always are, were soon on familiar terms with the boatmen, who told them that in former times many of the canoes were hollowed out of the trunks of cottonwood-trees.

The boys learned, too, that the Panama native Indian is a natural sportsman. Parrots, monkeys, pigeons, and small deer are his favourite game. His life is a very simple one. Nature provides him with bread in the shape of bananas and plantains. He makes his own pottery from the clay beneath his feet, and in place of knives and spoons uses gourds cut into proper shape.

He sleeps in a hammock or on a couch of bamboo with hides thrown over it. The hammocks are woven by the women.

All the time the boat was making good progress, and about four o'clock in the afternoon arrived at Palo Grande. On inquiry, it was learned that Señor Herreras lived about two miles west of the river, and after securing definite directions as to the route our friends started to walk to the plantation.

To Vasco, as well as to Harlan, the sights along the way were of special interest, for he knew nothing of country life. The growing corn, tobacco, indigo, coffee, vanilla beans, and other products of the country were a source of wonder to him. Even Mr. Andrews could well believe, with a former visitor to Panama, that "here it would puzzle a healthy man to die of hunger."

In less than an hour Señor Herreras's plantation was reached. It was now Vasco's turn to serve as guide and leader of the party. Finding his uncle at home, he introduced him to his friends, and told him of their desire for food and lodging.

"It is with great pleasure I welcome you all to my humble home," said the señor. "Will you kindly follow me within that you may rest after your long walk, and I will see that food is served to you at once. It is about our supper-hour, any way.

"And how is my sister, your mother?" Señor Herreras continued, addressing Vasco. "It has been many a long year since I have seen her."

"She is very well indeed, uncle, and it is because she told me of you that I am here with these friends. She said you would be sure to give us a royal welcome."

"And glad I am you took her advice. I only wish she were with you. Sometime I hope I may get down to the great city to see her."

Meanwhile, all had stepped within the house. The visitors were given an opportunity to remove the travel-stains, and by the time this had been done they were ready for the food which was set before them.

Vasco was specially glad to find that here were two cousins of about his own age, Jago and Alfeo, and before long the four boys were very well acquainted with each other.

The meal ended, Vasco's uncle inquired of Mr. Andrews as to his plans for the next day.

"I intend to go on up the river to Alhajuela, where I have some business in connection with the canal work."

"Did you expect to take the boys with you?"

"That was my plan."

"Well, why not let them stay here until you return. I will agree to take good care of them, and my boys will show them all about this place. I am sure they would all have a fine time — perhaps better than if they went with you, for boys love boy company."

"You may be right," said Mr. Andrews, "and I think I will accept your generous invitation on behalf of the boys. This is Wednesday, and I shall probably get back here Friday."

"Very well, then, we will consider that settled," said the host.

Early the next morning Mr. Andrews resumed his journey, Vasco's uncle providing a horse and accompanying him as far as the river.

Thus the four lads were left to their own devices.

"Let's take the boys down to the sugar-mill first," said Alfeo to his brother.

"That's a good idea," was Jago's reply, and Vasco and Harlan readily fell in with the suggestion.

Vasco's uncle raised much sugar-cane on his plantation, and in this mill he also did grinding for neighbours who were less fortunate and were unable to possess mills of their own.

Harlan found that the "mill" was not at all like what he imagined, and he regarded it as rather a small affair, but Vasco was immenselyimpressed with the wonderful work it performed.

It consisted of three upright cylinders of very hard wood, two of them about five feet long and one in the centre two feet higher. They were set close to each other, and a crude cog-wheel made the three revolve together.

An arm from the top of the central cylinder extended outward about fifteen feet. To this oxen were attached. Round and round in a circle the animals walked, and as they did so the machinery revolved. The stalks of cane were fed between the cylinders, and the heavy pressure squeezed out the juice, which fell into a large tub below.

Near by the boys saw the juice boiled. A great iron kettle was set in rough stone masonry, and dried cane was used for fuel. The boiling process was watched by an old woman, who was constantly dipping up the syrup with a long-handled gourd dipper.

Vasco and Harlan were each given a drink of the partially boiled cane-juice, which they found very pleasant to the taste.

"After the boiling is completed," the old woman told them, "the sugar is run into wooden moulds and then wrapped in plantain leaves, when it is ready for the market."

Harlan and Vasco were next taken to visit an aged woman who in years gone by had been a cook in Señor Herreras's father's household. This woman was said to be nearly a century old, and could tell the boys much of the ancient customs and habits of Panama.

The house in which she lived was like many of the native huts. It was very simply built. Four trees about six inches in diameter had been cut down, the branches lopped off, and a Y-shaped fork left at the tops. These four trees were set deep into the earth as corner posts. Side pieces were lashed on top with withes. The roof was made of small saplings thatched with native grasses, bunches of which overlapped each other like shingles.

In this particular hut there were two rooms, and an attic overhead, though many houses have no upper room. The sides of the hut were made of plaited split bamboo, and the chinks were filled with mud.

The old woman always welcomed the visits of Jago and Alfeo, and she was also glad to see the two young strangers. They found it easy to enter into conversation with her. She told how the Indians in her youthful days used to adorn their bodies with figures of birds, beasts, and trees. The women did the painting and took great delight in it. The men also wore a crescent-shaped metal plate over the lip, attached to the nose, and the women wore a ring in the same manner.

"What were the rings made of?" asked Vasco.

"Sometimes of gold, but more often of silver or of some cheaper metal," replied the woman. "Chains of animals' teeth and shell were also common.

"You would have laughed to see how the men used to smoke tobacco," continued the old woman. "Instead of a cigar, or even a pipe, long strips of tobacco leaf were wound into a roll two or three feet long and as large as your wrist.

"A boy would light one end of the roll and burn it to a coal, wetting the leaf next the fire to keep it from wasting too fast. The lighted end he put in his mouth and blew smoke through the roll into the face of each man in the company, no matter how many of them. Then they, sitting down as usual, with their hands made a kind of funnel around their mouths and noses. Into this they received the smoke as it was blown upon them, snuffing it greedily and strongly as long as they could hold their breath. It seemed to give them great pleasure."

"I don't think I should have liked the boy's task," said Vasco.

"Did the boys go hunting when you were young?" asked Alfeo.

"Oh, yes. They did not have guns for weapons, but used bows and arrows. They could shoot very straight with them, too. Just wait a moment and I will prove that to you."

The old woman hobbled to a chest in the corner of the room and took therefrom an old bamboo cane.

"Do you see the cleft in the end of that cane?" she asked.

"Yes, I do," answered Alfeo.

"Well, that was split by an arrow shot at twenty paces by my oldest brother when he was only eight years old."

The boys now took leave of the old woman, and the rest of the day they spent visiting various points of interest in the vicinity of the plantation. They also fished and went in swimming in a small stream which flowed near by and emptied into the Chagres.

At nightfall, four tired but happy boys were glad to get an early supper and seek the rest which a day of unusual activity demanded.

The next day, according to his plan, Mr. Andrews returned and remained overnight with Vasco's hospitable uncle.

Early Saturday morning, amid profuse expressions of regret at their departure and with invitations to come again, the travellers took up their journey homeward. This was made without special incident and was completed in safety.

CHAPTER XI.

NEW AMBITION

"DID you have a good time on your trip with Harlan and his father?" asked Lieutenant Barretas of Vasco.

"To be sure I did," was the answer. "I am not likely ever to forget the sights I have seen in this journey through our country."

"I hope you thanked your American friends for the pleasure you have enjoyed."

"I did, father."

"Our people are much indebted to the Americans for the prosperity into which we have come. I have some more good news to tell you now."

"What is it?" asked Vasco, his face aglow with eager anticipation.

"To-morrow a public school is to be opened, and I have decided that you shall attend."

This conversation occurred on Sunday, the day after Vasco's arrival home. The lieutenant was making his usual Sunday visit with his family, though he had come a little late on account of army affairs that had called him to the Blue House—the President's mansion. It was there that he had learned about the school.

Vasco received the information with a doubtful smile. A few weeks before he would have been sad to hear such a suggestion. But his acquaintance with Harlan, and especially the close companionship of the past week, had wrought certain changes in his spirit, and a dawning ambition had begun to arise within him.

He had come to see that there was a world different from that in which he had lived,—that his friend Harlan was of that world,—andthat the key to that world was knowledge. And knowledge, he knew, could be obtained only by hard labour. Was it worth the effort?

That was the question Vasco asked himself as he stood before his father.

To his credit be it said that his answer was the right one.

"I am glad of the chance," at last he told his father. "You may be sure that I shall try to make the best of it."

Let it be said here that this opportunity to go to school was a result of the formation of the new republic of Panama. One of the provisions of its constitution is: "Primary instruction shall be compulsory, and, when public, shall be free. There shall also be schools of arts and trades."

Monday morning Vasco and his sister Inez together started for school. To them, thus far, the institution was but a name, vague in its meaning, but full of great possibilities.

May we not well leave our little Panama cousin right here, as he stands on the threshold of a new life, under the folds of a new flag, with a new ambition and an earnest purpose spurring him on to attain to a higher and better life than he has ever known?

THE END.